W9-DGX-249

THE SUBSTITUTE TEACHER FROM THE
BLACK LAGOON

STORY BY
MIKE THALER

PICTURES BY
JARED LEE

Cartwheel
·B·O·O·K·S·®

SCHOLASTIC INC.

New York   Toronto   London   Auckland   Sydney
Mexico City   New Delhi   Hong Kong   Buenos Aires

For Emily and my new family with love.—M.T.
To Sue Watson Burmann, cheerleader and friend.—J.L.

visit us at www.abdopublishing.com

Reinforced library bound edition published in 2014 by Spotlight, a division of the ABDO Group, PO Box 398166, Minneapolis, MN 55439. Spotlight produces high-quality reinforced library bound editions for schools and libraries. Published by agreement with Scholastic, Inc.

Printed in the United States of America, North Mankato, Minnesota.
102013
012014

 This book contains at least 10% recycled materials.

Cataloging-in-Publication Data

Thaler, Mike, 1936-
  The substitute teacher from the black lagoon / by Mike Thaler ; pictures by Jared Lee.
  p. cm. -- (Black Lagoon)
  Summary: An elementary school class must contend with a substitute teacher that seems like the monster Frankenstein.
  1. Substitute teachers--Fiction. 2. Fear--Fiction. 3. Schools--Fiction.] I. Title. II Series.
  PZ7.T3 Sub 2005
  [E]--dc23

ISBN 978-1-61479-199-7 (Reinforced Library Bound Edition)

All Spotlight books are reinforced library binding and manufactured in the United States of America.

Mrs. Green is sick today.
I didn't know teachers got sick, too.
And we're going to have a sub.

Whoopee! This should be fun! We'll have recess all day, except for one hour, which will be for the party.

And we won't have any homework except playing video games
and watching TV. We can all chew gum, tell jokes, throw spitballs,
and dance on our desks.

We've got the lesson plan hidden and the blackboard erased, and all the books are buried. In an emergency, we have laughing gas and a book on *hippotism*.

Before noon, we'll have our substitute
stuffed and mounted on the bulletin board.

I hear footsteps coming down the hall.
We all look toward the door....

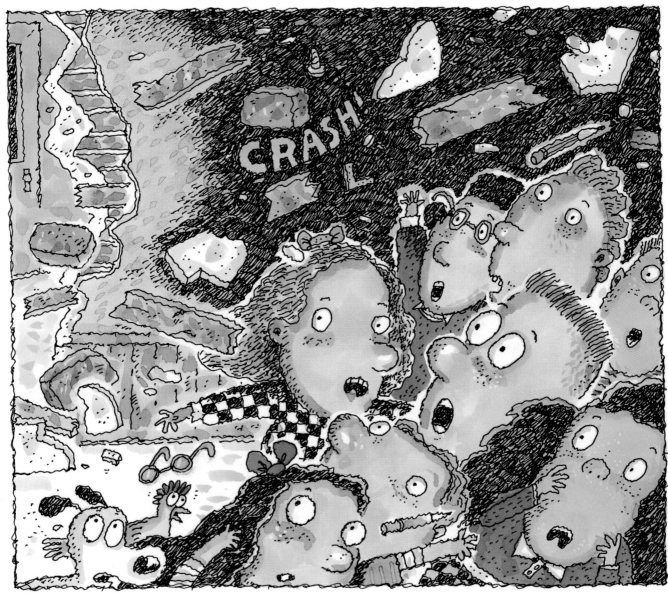

Suddenly, there's a crash!
The door doesn't open....

He comes in through the wall!
This is not a good sign.

He's nine feet tall,
and his arms are full of books.

As the dust settles, he writes his name on the chalkboard—
Frank N. Stein. The late bell rings.

We all jump up. "It's time for recess," we shout.
He turns around and growls—we all sit down.

Mr. Stein opens a math book.

"We never have math on Wednesday," shouts Derek.

"Let's try a little subtraction," grunts Mr. Stein, picking him up.
I guess that's a joke...*sub-traction*.

"If there are fifteen students and one disappears, how many are left?"
Derek counts on his fingers. "Fourteen," he stutters.
"Good," says Mr. Stein, setting him down.

FRENCH FRIES

CHICKEN LEG

"It's lunchtime!" shouts Randy, setting the clock hands to noon.
Mr. Stein comes over, lifts him up, and asks,

MOON

EARTH

"How would you like to go to the moon?"

"Not before noon," says Randy.

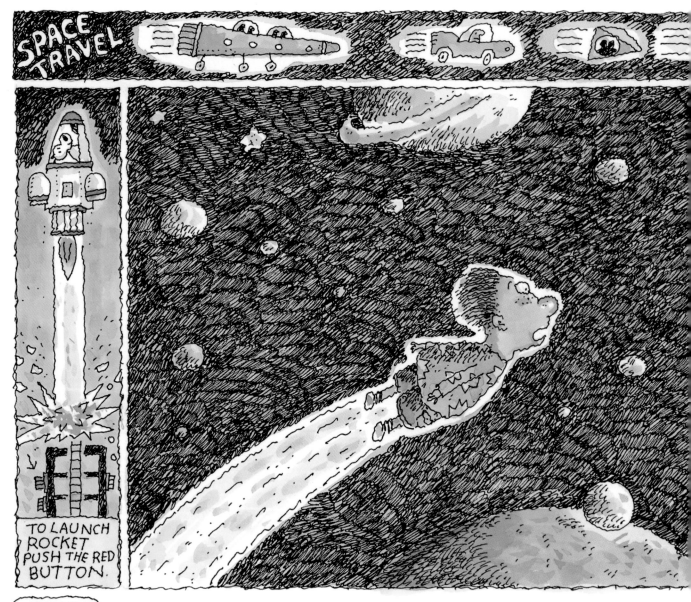

"Oh, I thought you said *launchtime*," says Mr. Stein, grinning.

I like a teacher with a sense of humor.

MOON WORM BANANA WITCH'S FINGERNAIL

"Well," says Mr. Stein, "let's try some geography. What state are we in now?"

TEXAS →

"A state of anxiety," stutters Randy.

 ← INDIANA

Mr. Stein smiles. "And what state can you wear?" he asks.

"Da-coat-a," says Eric.

"What about Pants-ylvania?" asks Mr. Stein with a smile.

"Say, why don't we make a state riddle book?"

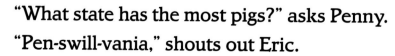

"What state has the most pigs?" asks Penny.
"Pen-swill-vania," shouts out Eric.

PIGGYBACK

PIGHEADED

PIGSKIN

"What about Boar-egon?"
answers Mr. Stein, laughing.

PIGTAILS

THE GREAT STATE RIDDLE BOOK by THE CLASS FROM THE BLACK LAGOON

Well, we make up a great state riddle book, illustrate it, and make a cardboard cover. We even miss recess to finish it because Mr. Stein isn't coming back tomorrow.

① WHAT IS THE HAPPIEST STATE?

HA. HA. HA.

ARF. ARF.

MERRY-LAND

② WHAT STATE DOES THE MOST LAUNDRY?

WASHING-TON

③ WHAT STATE LIKES COURT GAMES?

TENNIS-SEE

④ WHAT STATES HAVE THE MOST COWS?

COW-LIFORNIA AND MOO-SOURI

I'll miss him, but we dedicated the book to him
and proudly put it in the school library.
And every time I read it, I think of him.